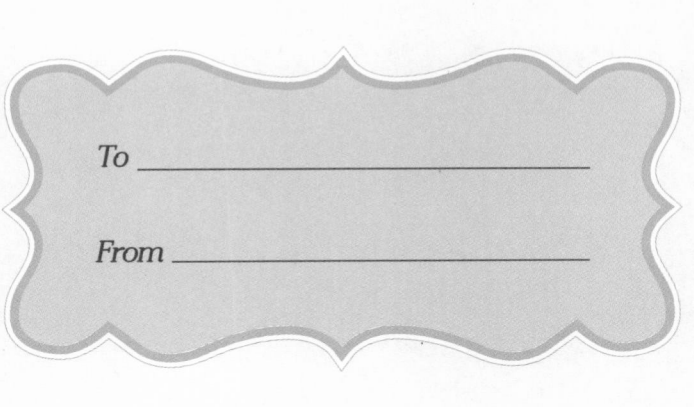

To _____

From _____

The Berenstain Bears

Bedtime Devotional

Includes 90 Devotions

by Mike Berenstain

Living Lights™
A Faith Story

ZONDER**kidz**

ZONDERKIDZ

The Berenstain Bears'® Bedtime Devotional
Copyright © 2016 by Berenstain Publishing, Inc.
Illustrations © 2016 by Berenstain Publishing, Inc.

Requests for information should be addressed to:
Zonderkidz, 3900 Sparks Dr. SE, Grand Rapids, Michigan 49546

ISBN 978-0-310-75165-6

Editor: Mary Hassinger
Contributor: Crystal Bowman
Design: Cindy Davis

Printed in China

18 19 20 21 /LPC/ 9 8 7 6 5 4

Table of Contents

Good Night, God

Oh God, Most Holy, Lord of All,
I praise your name, to you, I call!
Your loving care is always there.
I praise your name, in this nighttime prayer.

Sometimes my choices were not good,
I did not do the things I should.
But in your arms I come to rest.
You are forgiving, you are the best!

Thank you, Lord, for all things good.
I hope I thank you like I should.
Plants and animals, family and friends,
Books, school, and homes, there is no end.

The stars come out, our day is done,
I praise you, Lord, Most Holy One.
You give me fun and food and friends
And love from you that never ends.

God Loves You
Very Much

*It is good to sing every morning
about your love.* —Psalm 92:2

Morning Songs

Sister Bear is poking her head out the window to take a deep breath of the crisp morning air. She feels the warm sun on her face and listens to the birds as they sing happy songs. Do you ever listen to the birds sing their morning songs? Have you ever felt the warm sun on your face? God made the sun and the birds. He made the air that we breathe. He made them for you to enjoy because he loves you.

> *Sister's Prayer*
> *Thank you, Lord, for birds that sing,*
> *praising you for everything.*

The Lord is good to all. He shows deep concern for everything he has made. —Psalm 145:9

Tender Care

Sister Bear is holding a baby bunny. Maybe the bunny is hungry and needs a carrot to munch. Sister will take care of the bunny until he can hop away to find his bunny friends. God made all the animals and he takes care of them. He helps bunnies and bears and elephants find food to eat and water to drink. He helps birds build nests in the trees. He sends rain to fill the ponds so ducks have a place to swim. God cares for everything he made, including you.

Brother's Prayer
Thank you for your tender care.
Bless all creatures everywhere.

11

His love is as high as the heavens
are above the earth. —Psalm 103:11

How High?

Sister Bear and her friend Suzy are looking at the moon and the stars high in the sky. Have you ever looked at the moon and the stars? Do you wonder how far away they are? You can see them but you cannot reach them. They are way too high! The Bible says God's love is so high it reaches all the way to the sky. God loves you with a love that is higher than the highest star. Remember to thank God for his love that is so high.

Carry On, Cub!

Before you close your eyes tonight, think a little bit about God's love. It is so good to be loved this much! So, how can you show God you are thankful for his love? Plan on thanking God all day, tomorrow. Wake up and tell God that every good thing you do all day long is to honor and thank him! Do something extra nice for others to show them how much you love them. Tell friends that God loves them too.

> <u>Sister's Prayer</u>
> *Thank you for your love so high,*
> *it reaches way up to the sky.*

The Lord is my shepherd. He gives me everything I need. —Psalm 23:1

Our Shepherd

Brother likes to read Bible stories about David the shepherd boy. David took good care of his sheep. He would help them find food to eat and places to rest. He would protect them from danger while they were sleeping. David wrote many of the Psalms that are in the Bible too. In Psalm 23 David says that God is our shepherd because he watches over us and gives us what we need. God will keep us safe because he loves us just like a shepherd loves his sheep.

Carry On, Cub!

Before you close your eyes tonight, think a little bit about God's love. We all need to have someone take care of us sometimes. Isn't it great that God will take care of us no matter what? He only wants to know we are safe and happy. While you are out playing or at school working, be sure to think about how God is watching over you—no matter where you are or what you are doing. Be sure to thank him for that loving care and protection.

> **Brother's Prayer**
> *You're my shepherd, I'm your sheep.*
> *You keep me safe while I'm asleep.*

God so loved the world that he gave his one and only Son.
Anyone who believes in him will not die but will have eternal life.
—John 3:16

The Greatest Love

The Bear cubs love Christmas. But it's not just the presents they love. They love the story of how God sent his son Jesus to be born as a baby. When Jesus grew up, he told people that God loved them. Some people didn't like what Jesus said so they hung him on a cross until he died. But Jesus came back to life and went to heaven. Jesus died on the cross for our sins. There is no greater love than that! You can thank Jesus for his love all year long.

Brother's Prayer
Jesus, you took my sins away.
Thank you for that special day.

So we know that God loves us.
We depend on it. —1 John 4:16

You Can Know

Brother and Sister like reading all the stories in the Bible. They like learning about God and his promises. Do you have a Bible that someone reads to you? Or maybe you can read it by yourself. You can learn many things from the Bible. The Bible tells us over and over that God loves us very much. You never have to wonder if God loves you. You can know for sure that God loves you because he says so. God loves you every minute of every day!

Sister's Prayer
Your love for me is great I know
because the Bible tells me so.

17

See what amazing love the Father has given us!
Because of it, we are called children of God. —1 John 3:1

God's Family

The Bear family has five in their family. How many people do you have in your family? Some families are big and some are small. Sometimes grandpas and grandmas or aunts and uncles are part of a family too. No matter what size family you have, you can be part of God's big family too. God loves you so much he wants you to be his child. You can be part of God's family by believing in Jesus.

Carry On, Cub!

Before you close your eyes tonight, think a little bit about God's love. Being a part of a family is so important. Being a part of God's family—a child of God—is most important! He has so much love that everyone can be a part of his family and no one needs to worry if he has enough love. It goes on and on. How do you show your family that you love them? Tell the people in your family how much you love them tomorrow. And tell God you love him too!

<u>Honey Bear's Prayer</u>
Thank you for families, big or small.
Lord, I know you love us all.

"Let the little children come to me. Don't keep them away. The kingdom of heaven belongs to people like them." —Matthew 19:14.

Come to Jesus

Brother and Sister are saying their bedtime prayers. Do you say a special prayer at bedtime or when you eat your dinner? Jesus loves it when children pray to him. When Jesus lived on earth he said, "Let the children come to me!" Jesus placed his hands on their heads and blessed them. Jesus wants you to come to him too. You can do that by saying a prayer or reading the Bible. You can come to Jesus by singing a song to him. Jesus loves children all over the world!

Carry On, Cub!

Before you close your eyes tonight, think a little bit about God's love. Jesus showed the people around him that they mattered to him. He touched them. He smiled. He taught them about how much his Father loves them. He teaches us all of that too. And he showed the world how great his love is by dying on the cross for our sins. How will you show Jesus you love him tomorrow? Will you say a good morning prayer to him? Will you smile at mom and dad and tell them you love them? Will you help someone at school? Or one of your brothers or sisters at home? All of your actions tomorrow should show Jesus how much you love him.

Brother's Prayer
Jesus, I come to you today;
I am near you when I pray.

"Be still, and know that I am God."
—Psalm 46:10

Be Still

Sister is standing very still. She is looking at a pretty butterfly God made. Have you ever stopped to look at a butterfly? Do you ever just stand still to look at the sky and the clouds and the sun? Maybe if you are very quiet you can hear birds singing. Sometimes God wants us to be quiet for a while so we can see and hear all the wonderful things he made for us to enjoy. Everything God made shows us how much he loves us.

Carry On, Cub!

Before you close your eyes tonight, think a little bit about God's love. Think about God's creation. What do you see? Grass and trees? Birds and furry animals? Bugs and flowers? Your mom and your best friend? Can you hear the singing birds, the buzzing bees, and the whooshing wind? Everything you see and hear shows how much God loves us. Tomorrow take some time to notice God's creation around you and your home. Take a few minutes to thank him for these great gifts. Promise God that you will respect his creation—all of that shows God how much you love him.

Sister's Prayer
Help me, God, to stop and see
the wonderful things you made for me.

The LORD is good. His faithful love continues forever.
—Psalm 100:5

Forever and Ever

Brother and Sister want to play outside, but it's raining. Have you ever had to stay inside because of the rain? The good news is that rain doesn't last forever. When the rain finally stops you can go outside to play. Did you know there is something that does last forever? It's God's love. The Bible tells us that God will never stop loving us. His love will last forever and ever and ever. And that's good news!

Carry On, Cub!

Before you close your eyes tonight, think a little bit about God's love. If something is forever what does that mean? It means that something will never, ever stop. God's love is forever. No matter how old we get, how far away we go, how tall we grow, or what we do, God's love for us will just keep going. Take a few minutes during your new day to thank God for his forever love. Let him know you will love him forever too.

> ### Brother's Prayer
> *Jesus, I come to you today;*
> *I am near you when I pray.*

Be Kind and
Helpful to Others

Love your neighbor as you love yourself.
—Matthew 22:39

Love Your Neighbor

The Bears are kind to their neighbors. When someone isn't feeling too well, Brother and Sister will bring some lunch and lemonade. Do you have people in your neighborhood? When any of your neighbors are sick or sad, you can be kind to them too. You can make a card for them or bring them something to eat. Sometimes it's nice to just stop by and say hi. Jesus wants us to love our neighbors. When we show kindness to them, we are showing God's love.

Brother's Prayer
Help me to be kind and good
to others in my neighborhood.

A gentle answer turns anger away.
But mean words stir up anger. —Proverbs 15:1

Kind Words

Brother and Sister are saying mean things to each other. They are not being kind. That's not how God wants us to treat others. Did you know you can be kind with your words? If someone says mean words to you, it's easy to say mean words back. But if you stop and ask God to help you, you can say kind words instead. When you say kind words, the other person might stop being mean to you. Kind words are always better than mean words.

> *Brother's Prayer*
> *Help me use kind words today.*
> *Kind words are the best to say.*

Let us not become tired of doing good.
—Galatians 6:9

Don't Quit

Brother and Sister are working to help clean up the yard. Working in the yard is hard and can make you tired. Maybe you help your mom or dad inside the house by cleaning your room or setting the table. That's hard work too! Even if you feel like quitting, it's best to keep working until the job is finished. Helping your parents is a way to show kindness to them. You might get tired, but it feels good to be a helper.

Carry On, Cub!

Before you close your eyes tonight, think a little bit about being kind. Sometimes being kind to someone is as simple as smiling at a friend. Sometimes it is as easy as waving hello. And sometimes being kind can be doing something that's hard or messy or long like raking leaves or shoveling snow for a neighbor. Whatever you choose to do, decide that tomorrow you will show someone kindness. It will make them and God smile!

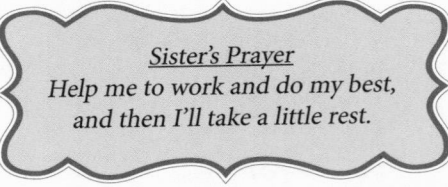

Sister's Prayer
Help me to work and do my best,
and then I'll take a little rest.

Be kind and tender to one another.
—Ephesians 4:32

Sister and Lizzy like fishing together. Sister is giving Lizzy a little hug, just to let her know how much she likes being her friend and spending time together. Do you like it when someone gives you a hug? It's nice to get hugs, but it's nice to give hugs too. You can hug your mom or dad. You can hug your grandpa or grandma. You can even give a hug to your brother or sister. When you give those you love a little hug or show them you like spending time with them, it puts a big smile on every face.

Carry On, Cub!

Before you close your eyes tonight, think a little bit about being kind. There are many ways to show someone you care about them. There are many ways to show kindness to others. Simple things like a smile, a wave, a pat on the back, or a hug for your mom or best friend are easy and fast and mean so much to people. In the Bible we read about how Jesus showed his love by touching people to heal them. So tomorrow, be like Jesus. Put a smile on your face or your arms around a friend and be kind.

Sister's Prayer
A little hug is just one way
that I can show your love today.

Do to others as you want them to do to you.
—Luke 6:31

A Good Rule

Billy wants to help Brother fly his fancy airplane.
Brother isn't sure that's a good idea. But then he
remembers we are supposed to treat others the way
we want to be treated, so Brother decides to have
Billy help him. Do you want others to be kind to
you? Then it's important that you treat others with
kindness. The Bible says, "Do to others as you want
them to do to you." That's called the Golden Rule,
and it's a good rule to follow!

> <u>Brother's Prayer</u>
> *Help me to follow the Golden Rule*
> *when I'm at home or church or school.*

Dear children, don't just talk about love. Put your love into action. Then it will truly be love. —1 John 3:18

Let it Show

Sister is asking Suzy to play with her at recess. She saw Suzie sitting all by herself and wants her to join in the fun. It's nice to tell someone you love them, but it's also important to show it. When we are kind, it shows others we love them because we love Jesus. When you see someone who is playing alone, you can ask them to play with you. You can have lots of fun together and you might even make a new friend.

Sister's Prayer
Help me to work and do my best,
and then I'll take a little rest.

*Always try to do what is good for each other
and for everyone else.* —1 Thessalonians 5:15

Good for Everyone

The Bears have some neighbors who are a little different. They speak and even dress differently from other folks the Bear cubs are used to seeing. But they are good neighbors and good friends. They help each other out too. When you do nice things for others, it's good for them and it's good for you. Being a helper in your neighborhood and being kind to kids at school is what God wants you to do. It's the best thing for everyone!

Carry On, Cub!

Before you close your eyes tonight, think a little bit about being kind. Are there kids at school who sometimes need help? Maybe your friend has a heavy backpack. Maybe a classmate has a broken leg and needs help with her lunch tray. Whatever way you can help, you should. When you make someone happy you usually feel happier too. Jesus tried to help everyone who needed him. Tomorrow you can be like Jesus and be helpful to someone in need.

*<u>Honey Bear's Prayer</u>
Being kind and helpful too
is what you want us all to do.*

Children, obey your parents in everything.
That pleases the Lord. —Colossians 3:20

Obey Your Parents

The Bears are going for a walk on a sunny afternoon. Brother and Sister are walking too fast and getting too far ahead. Mama and Papa want them to slow down. Do you think Brother and Sister should listen to them? God made families so that grownups can take care of their children. God wants kids to listen to their parents. It's their job to keep their children safe. Your parents know what's best for you. When you listen to them, you please your parents and you also please God.

> *Sister's Prayer*
> *Help me to listen and obey*
> *so I will please you, Lord, today.*

So put on tender mercy and kindness as if they were your clothes. —Colossians 3:12

Special Clothes

Brother and Sister are ready for their soccer game. They are wearing their soccer uniforms to show what team they belong to. If you play sports, you might have a special outfit or T-shirt to wear to your games too. Did you know the Bible talks about special clothes? The Bible tells us to wear kindness just like we wear clothes. When you get dressed in the morning, think about being kind to others all day long. When you wear kindness, it shows you belong to God.

> ### Brother's Prayer
> *Kindness is what I need to wear.*
> *Help me, Lord, to show I care.*

Kind words are like honey. They are sweet to the spirit and bring healing to the body. —Proverbs 16:24

Sweet as Honey

Honey Bear's name fits her well because she loves sweet treats. Candy, ice cream, and pumpkin pie always put a smile on her face. Kids like sweet treats, but healthy food is better for your body. Did you know the Bible says words can be sweet too? When we speak words of kindness, they are sweet like honey. They make others feel good and happy inside. And the good thing about kind words is they are healthy for your body!

Carry On, Cub!

Before you close your eyes tonight, think a little bit about kind words. What are kind words? Some examples are: Hello!, Have a great day!, That's a nice hat, Good job on the story you wrote, You are a good soccer player. Thanks for breakfast, Mom.

When you speak kind words you make a person smile. They feel good. You will feel good. God will be so happy. Speak kind words tomorrow.

<u>Honey Bear's Prayer</u>
*Make my words be kind and sweet
to bless my family with a treat.*

Be Forgiving

Scripture says, "Everyone who calls on the name of the Lord will be saved." —Romans 10:13

Jesus Saves

Every Sunday the Bear family goes to church. They like to sing songs, read the Bible, and learn more about God. We can learn a lot from the Bible. The most important lesson in the Bible is that God loves us and sent his Son, Jesus, to die on the cross for our sins. When we tell Jesus we love him and ask him to forgive our sins, he will. Then we will be with Jesus in heaven someday. That's what it means to be saved.

<u>Brother's Prayer</u>
Jesus, I believe you came to save all those who call your name.

But God is faithful and fair. If we confess our sins, he will forgive our sins. He will forgive every wrong thing we have done. He will make us pure. —1 John 1:9

Tell God

Sister is thanking God for keeping her safe today. She is also telling God about something she did wrong. She is asking God to forgive her. When we do something wrong, it's called sin. You might tell a lie or say a bad word or be mean to someone at school. Those are things God doesn't want us to do. But here's the good part—if you tell God you are sorry for your sins, he will forgive you because he loves you. God's forgiveness makes us pure.

> *Sister's Prayer*
> *Please forgive me of my sin.*
> *Help me to be pure again.*

You will throw all our sins into the bottom of the sea. —Micah 7:19

At the Bottom

The Bears are going for a walk in the woods. They see a big pond and wonder how deep it is. If Brother throws a stone into the pond and it sinks to the bottom, he will not get it back. That's what God's forgiveness is like. The Bible says when God forgives our sins it's like he throws them into the sea and they go down to the bottom. That means our sins are gone forever. God forgives our sins because he loves us.

Carry On, Cub!

Before you close your eyes tonight, think a little bit about forgiveness. It is a great gift that God forgives our sins. Not only does he forgive us, but then he says, "Ok, now start all over. Try hard to be good." And if we sin again and are sorry, God will forgive us again! Tomorrow, tell God thank you for his forgiveness.

Brother's Prayer
You throw my sins into the sea.
You take them far away from me.

Everyone has sinned. No one measures up to God's glory. —Romans 3:23

Nobody's Perfect

Brother is trying to stop a fight at school. One student is being a troublemaker, but the other one is causing problems too. Do you know kids who sometimes get into trouble? Some people mess up, sometimes a lot! But even people who are good most of the time are not perfect. The Bible says everyone sins and no one is perfect. We all need to tell God we are sorry for the wrong things we do. Then we can ask God to forgive us and help us do what is right.

Carry On, Cub!

Before you close your eyes tonight, think a little bit about forgiveness. God knows we are not perfect. Not one friend you know is perfect. Only God is perfect. So when we do something wrong God is not angry. He knows there are times we all make mistakes. But he wants you to ask him for forgiveness. Do that and he will be happy.

> **Brother's Prayer**
> *Lord, I'm asking you tonight*
> *to help me try and do what's right.*

Blessed is the person whose sin the Lord never counts against them. —Psalm 32:2

It Doesn't Count

Brother and Sister are counting how many lines they have to learn for their play. They will practice a lot so they can remember their lines. What things do you like to count? Do you count your markers or crayons when you put them back in the box? Do you count the days until it's your birthday? The Bible tells us about something that God never counts. He never counts our sins. Instead of counting our sins, he forgives them so we can be saved.

Sister's Prayer
Thank you, God, for I am blessed.
Your forgiveness is the best.

Forgive one another, just as God forgave you because of what Christ has done. —Ephesians 4:32

Forgive Others

Brother and Sister are walking to school. They are happy and talking to each other. But at breakfast they were not smiling. They fought over who would get the last bowl of cereal and said some mean words to each other. Mama made them apologize and talked to the cubs about forgiving each other. Do you know why we need to forgive others? It's because God forgives us. When we do things that are wrong, God will forgive us when we tell him we are sorry. God wants us to forgive others just like he forgives us.

> **Brother's Prayer**
> Lord, you forgive, so I will too.
> I will show my love for you.

But Joseph said to them, "Don't be afraid. Do you think I'm God? You planned to harm me. But God planned it for good. —Genesis 50:

A Good Story

Papa is reading a Bible story to Brother and Sister before they go to sleep. He is reading the story of Joseph and his brothers from the Old Testament. Joseph's brothers were mean to him. They sent him away and thought he was gone for good. When they saw him again, many years later, the brothers thought Joseph would be mean to them. But Joseph was kind and forgave his brothers. He knew God used him in a special way. God can help us forgive people who are mean to us. He will even help us to love them.

Carry On, Cub!

Before you close your eyes tonight, think a little bit about forgiveness. Has anyone ever said they were sorry to you? Was it hard to tell that person that everything would be OK? Sometimes we do not want to forgive. Sometimes we think we want to stay upset. But God does not want us to be upset. He wants us to forgive others as he forgives us! Tomorrow, try to be like God. Be forgiving if someone has hurt you.

Sister's Prayer
Help me to love and to forgive.
Help me to please you as I live.

And forgive us our sins, just as we also have forgiven those who sin against us. —Matthew 6:12

A Special Prayer

Brother is saying a special prayer tonight. He knows a prayer from the Bible called the Lord's Prayer. It's called the Lord's Prayer because it's the prayer Jesus said when he was teaching his followers how to pray. One part of the prayer talks about forgiveness. It's about asking God to forgive us just like we should forgive others. If we want God to forgive us, then we need to forgive others. When we forgive others, it shows God how much we love him.

Carry On, Cub!

Before you close your eyes tonight, think a little bit about forgiveness. Promise yourself that tomorrow you will show God how much you love him. Promise that you will be forgiving if someone hurts you. Promise that you will thank God for forgiving you.

Brother's Prayer
*Forgiving others is what I'll do,
I know that you'll forgive me too.*

Most of all, love one another deeply.
Love erases many sins by forgiving them. —1 Peter 4:8

Lots of Love

Sometimes Brother and Sister get on each other's nerves. Sometimes they tease each other and say mean things. Sometimes they even yell at each other. But the truth is they really love each other. When Brother and Sister remember to show love to each other, it helps them forget about the times they don't get along. Do you have a brother or sister or friend who gets on your nerves sometimes? Just remember to show them lots of love. Soon you'll forget about the rest.

Carry On, Cub!

Before you close your eyes tonight, think a little bit about forgiveness. If you love someone, you want them to be happy. You want them to know they are important to you no matter what. So even if your brother, sister, or friend hurt you, you need to be like God and forgive. It might not be easy, but it is the right thing to do.

Sister's Prayer
Help me to love instead of fight.
Show me how to do what's right.

No one has ever seen God. But if we love one another, God lives in us. His love is made complete in us. —1 John 4:12

Good Morning, God

The Bears will soon be waking up to see God's pretty sunrise. No one has ever seen God, but every day we can see all the beautiful things he has made. The Bible says when we are kind and loving to others, it shows that God is living in us. When we forgive people who hurt us and show love to them instead, they will know God is the one who helps us do that. With God's love inside of us, we can love everyone.

Carry On, Cub!

Before you close your eyes tonight, think a little bit about forgiveness. Tomorrow will be a great day to show someone how much you love and care for them. That might mean being forgiving if someone hurts you on the playground. It might mean helping your brother clean the bedroom even though it is his mess. If you show others kindness and love they will know God's love too.

> *Honey Bear's Prayer*
> *Help me to live so others can see your special love inside of me.*

God's Gifts
and Blessings

In the beginning, God created the heavens and the earth. —Genesis 1:1

God Made It All

The Bear family is going for a nature walk. They like to walk by the stream and look for animals. Do you ever go for a nature walk? When you go for a walk outside, you can see many things God made for us to enjoy. He made the warm sun and puffy clouds in the sky. He made the green grass and trees and bushes. He made birds and squirrels and black and yellow bumblebees. Every part of God's creation is his gift to us.

> *Honey Bear's Prayer*
> *Thank you, God, for birds and trees,*
> *for squirrels and grass and bumblebees.*

He gives those who are thirsty all the water they want.
He gives those who are hungry all the good food they can eat.
—Psalm 107:9

Delicious Blessings

The Bear family is sitting around the table with some of their friends. They are hungry and ready to eat some good food. Do you know where our food comes from? You might go to the store to buy it, but it really comes from God. God created the soil and the seeds that farmers plant. He made trees that give us apples and pears and oranges. He made bushes to give us blueberries, and plants to give us tomatoes. The food we eat and the water we drink are all blessings from God.

> *Sister's Prayer*
> *Bless our food and water too.*
> *Lord, these blessings come from you.*

May the Lord bless you and take good care of you.
—Numbers 6:24

Special Care

Honey Bear and Brother are going for a walk on a chilly morning. They are wearing their jackets to keep them warm. They like to go lots of places just like you do. If you go for a morning walk, you can ask God to keep you safe. When you're playing with your friends, you can ask God to bless you. At bedtime you can ask God to watch over you all night. Every day and night ask God to bless you and keep you in his special care.

Carry On, Cub!

Before you close your eyes tonight, think a little bit about God's blessings. When you wake up tomorrow thank God for giving you a new day! Ask him to keep you and your family safe. He wants us to ask him for blessings. He wants to know you need him and appreciate everything he has given you.

> <u>Brother's Prayer</u>
> Lord, you're with me everywhere.
> Keep me in your special care.

*We all have gifts. They differ according to
the grace God has given to each of us. —Romans 12:6*

Different Gifts

Brother and Sister like making Bible story pictures
when they go to Sunday school. Today they listened
to the story about Noah's ark. Do you like to draw
pictures and color them? Maybe you like to sing or
play soccer. God gives each of us different abilities
for doing certain things well. Some kids are good
artists. Some are good singers, and some are good
soccer ball kickers. The important thing is to use the
gifts God has given you to bless others and honor
him.

Carry On, Cub!

*Before you close your eyes tonight, think a little bit about
God's blessings. What blessings and gifts has he given you?
Can you run fast? Can you read a whole book or write a long
story? These gifts are called talents and God wants us to use
them. When we use our gifts we are showing God how much
we love him! How will you use your gifts tomorrow?*

> Sister's Prayer
> *You give us gifts to use each day
> while we work and while we play.*

My God will meet all your needs. He will meet them in keeping with his wonderful riches. —Philippians 4:19

Bless Our Home

Mama and Papa Bear have three cubs and a nice home. They have food to eat, water to drink, and beds to sleep in. They are happy and blessed. Some families live in houses. Some live in apartments or trailers. Some families share a home with their grandpa and grandma. No matter where you live, if you have food to eat and a place to sleep, you are blessed. Everything you have is a gift from God. He gives you what you need.

Honey Bear's Prayer
Thank you for my nice warm bed
where I can rest my sleepy head.

*Then the L*ORD *will send rain on your land at the right time. He'll send rain in the fall and in the spring. You will be able to gather your grain.* —Deuteronomy 11:14

Showers of Blessings

Brother and Sister and some of their friends were complaining about the rain. Preacher Brown tells them rain is a gift and blessing from God. God sends rain to water the grass and trees and flowers. He sends rain at the right time so crops will grow in the fields so there will be good food to eat. Rain gives us water to drink and makes everything clean. The next time it's raining, remember that rain is a gift from God.

<u>*Brother's Prayer*</u>
Even on the rainy days
I will give you all my praise.

*Give, and it will be given to you. . . . The same amount
you give will be measured out to you. —Luke 6:38*

Be a Blessing

Honey Bear is putting some money in a big pot. The
money from the pot will help families that need food
or clothes. God gives us lots of gifts and blessings.
He wants us to share what we have with others.
Maybe you have an extra pair of shoes or a jacket
that's too small. Do you have toys you can give to
kids who might not have any? You can even give
food to places that give hungry people food to eat.
Whenever you give to others, you are a blessing and
God will bless you back by loving you!

Carry On, Cub!

*Before you close your eyes tonight, think a little bit about
God's blessings. You are one of God's blessings! Yes, you are.
When you obey your mom. When you do your schoolwork on
time. When you help your neighbor with their recycling. When
you help a friend on the playground. You are a blessing. God
wants you to do all of those things and he wants you to do
more. Be helpful tomorrow. Be kind and generous and caring.
And God will bless you right back with his love.*

Honey Bear's Prayer
I will give and I will share.
I want to show how much I care.

The Lord gives wisdom. Knowledge and understanding come from his mouth. —Proverbs 2:6

Get Wisdom

Sister is ready to take her spelling test. She studied hard and will do her best. It's good to study and learn new things. God made our minds so we can learn about stars and planets and far away countries. We can learn about words and numbers and animals. And when we read the Bible we can learn about God. The Bible says that God gives us wisdom. Wisdom is knowing what to do at the right time. If you want wisdom, just ask God and he will give it to you.

Sister's Prayer
Wisdom is a gift from you.
Help me learn what's right and true.

Your word is like a lamp that shows me the way.
It is like a light that guides me. —Psalm 119:105

The Best Kind of Light

Papa is turning out the light. It's time for Brother and Sister to go to sleep. When the light is out, they need to stay in their beds or they might bump into something in the dark. Lights help us see where we are going so we don't get hurt or lost. Did you know the Bible is like a light? God gave us the Bible to help us know how to live. It lights the way for us and guides us so we can be safe. The Bible is the best kind of light.

Brother's Prayer
The Bible is a special light
that keeps me safe both day and night.

Every good and perfect gift is from God. This kind of gift comes down from the Father who created the heavenly lights. —James 1:17

The Perfect Gift

The Bears celebrate Christmas together. Brother picked out a gift for Sister, and Sister picked out a gift for Brother. They hope it's something good! Everyone likes to get gifts—especially "good" gifts. The Bible tells us about the best gift of all. It's the gift of Jesus who was born on Christmas day. Jesus is God's gift to us all year long. He came from heaven to earth to be our Savior. Jesus is more than a good gift. He is the perfect gift!

Carry On, Cub!

Before you close your eyes tonight, think a little bit about God's blessings. Remember, everything good comes from God. So that means you are a blessing—a gift from God to your family and friends and the world. But the greatest gift ever is Jesus! Tomorrow, thank God for the gift of his Son. Work hard to be worthy of the most perfect gift, the most special blessing.

> *Sister's Prayer*
> *Jesus, you came from heaven above*
> *to be God's perfect gift of love.*

Be Thankful

Give thanks to the Lord, because he is good.
His faithful love continues forever. —Psalm 136:1

God Is Good

Sister loves all kinds of animals. She likes butterflies and dogs, lizards and frogs. She even likes ladybugs. She knows that God takes care of the animals, just like he takes care of her. That's because God is good and full of love. God is good to us and everything he made. He helps animals find food to eat. He gives us homes and families. God does many good things every day. Remember to say thank you to God for his goodness.

> *Sister's Prayer*
> *Thank You, God—it's plain to see*
> *that you are very good to me.*

So my heart will sing your praises. I can't keep silent.
Lord, my God, I will praise you forever. —Psalm 30:12

Sing Out Loud

Papa is singing a song on the way to church. Brother and Sister aren't sure what to do, but Honey Bear sings right along. Papa is so thankful for God's love that he just can't help but sing! That's what it's like when you are thankful deep down in your heart. When you are thankful on the inside, it shows on the outside. If you want to thank God for his love, you can tell him with words, or you can sing it out loud for everyone to hear.

> <u>Honey Bear's Prayer</u>
> I will sing out loud and clear
> a song of thanks so all can hear.

Don't worry about anything. No matter what happens, tell God about everything. Ask and pray, and give thanks to him.
—Philippians 4:6

No More Worries

Mama is saying goodnight to Brother. He has a lot on his mind and is worried about tomorrow. Kids worry about things like school and friends, and grownups worry too. The Bible tells us not to worry. But if you do start to worry, you can tell God everything and he will listen. You can ask God to help you with your problems no matter how big or small they are. We can be thankful that God listens to us when we talk to him.

Carry On, Cub!

Before you close your eyes tonight, think a little bit about being thankful. Have you ever felt nervous or worried about something? Maybe you have a spelling test coming up. Maybe the first baseball game of the season is tomorrow. Or maybe you are wondering if dad will like the birthday gift you made him. If something makes you feel worried tomorrow remember one thing—God is there to help. No matter how big or small the worry is, he is right beside you. Be sure to thank him for his support and love!

Brother's Prayer
When I worry, I will pray.
You will listen right away.

Lord, I will praise you with all my heart.
—Psalm 138:1

A Thankful Heart

Sister is thankful for the way God made her. She likes to run and climb and swing. And she really likes to ice skate! What do you like to do? Some kids like to draw or paint pictures. Maybe you like to ride bikes or swim or play catch with a friend. Do you like to use your hands to build tall towers or sandcastles? Whatever you enjoy doing, be thankful that God made you to do so many different things.

Carry On, Cub!

Before you close your eyes tonight, think a little bit about being thankful. God made you just the way you are. You are perfect in his eyes. The things you can do, the way you look, and feel, and sound—all of those things come from God. Tomorrow is a good day to thank him for these gifts. So when you run tomorrow, run your fastest, when you play with your friends, be the best friend you can be, when you help your mom, work your hardest and show God you love how he made you and you are thankful.

<u>Sister's Prayer</u>
You made me in a special way,
so I can swing and laugh and play.

Give thanks no matter what happens. God wants you to thank him because you believe in Christ Jesus. —1 Thessalonians 5:18

No Matter What

Brother and Sister are walking home from school in the rain. At first they were not happy, but now they're having fun splashing in the puddles. Sometimes when things seem bad, they can turn out to be good. You might not be able to play outside on a cold and windy day, but you can enjoy reading books or playing games inside. God wants us to be thankful no matter what happens. On good days and even not so good days, you can be thankful that God loves you.

Brother's Prayer
No matter if days are good or bad,
help me, Lord, to be thankful and glad.

Give thanks as you enter the gates of his temple. Give praise as you enter its courtyards. Give thanks to him and praise his name. —Psalm 100:4

Brother and Sister are thankful they can go to church and praise God with their neighbors and friends. If you go to church, you can be thankful too. But even when you are not in church, you can praise God and thank him wherever you are. You can praise God on the playground while you ride the merry-go-round. You can thank him for your toys when you're cleaning your room. And you can thank God that you can talk to him anytime or anywhere.

> *Sister's Prayer*
> *I'm thankful I can talk to you*
> *at home, at church, and playgrounds too.*

Do everything you say or do in the name of the Lord Jesus. Always give thanks to God the Father through Christ. —Colossians 3:17

Thankful Helpers

Today Brother and Sister are going to help some neighbors fix their house. Brother can hand the hammer and nails to Papa, and Sister can carry the boards. They are thankful God made them strong and healthy so they can be helpers. Are you thankful you can be a helper? Maybe you can pick up trash or sticks in the yard. Maybe you can bring mail to a neighbor who is sick, or feed a neighbor's cat. Whatever you do, be thankful you can do it!

Carry On, Cub!

Before you close your eyes tonight, think a little bit about being thankful. Everyone needs a little help sometimes. And God wants us to do our best to be good helpers. He blesses each of us with ways that we can be helpful—from being good at cleaning to being good at reading to our little brothers and sisters. And we can thank God for these abilities by using them every chance we get.

<u>Brother's Prayer</u>
In everything I say and do,
I will give my thanks to you.

All creatures depend on you to give them their food
when they need it. —Psalm 104:27

Thank You, God

The Bears are getting ready to eat a delicious meal. They are thanking God for meat and potatoes and pumpkin pie. Do you remember to thank God for your food before you eat? When we thank God for our food, it helps us remember that God is the one who gives it to us. It's not a good feeling to be hungry all the time. If you have food to eat every day, then you can be thankful every day!

Carry On, Cub!

Before you close your eyes tonight, think a little bit about being thankful. You probably say thank you to mom or dad for making a delicious dinner. You say thank you to your friend who shares her lunch with you at school. But do you remember to pray and say thank you to God for your food every day? He is the creator who made the fruit trees, the vegetables, the animals, even the rain and soil that help them all grow. Tomorrow before dinner, say a prayer to God, thanking him for the gift of food to eat. Add a prayer for all the children who are hungry, that they will be fed as well.

Honey Bear's Prayer
Thank you, Lord, for food to eat,
for vegetables and fruit and meat.

Our God, we give you thanks. We praise your glorious name.
—1 Chronicles 29:13

See God's Glory

Sister will soon wake up to see the sunrise. Have you ever seen the sun come up in the morning? Maybe you've watched a sunset at the end of the day. Sometimes the sky has lots of pretty colors like red and pink and orange. The sky shows us God's glory. It shows us how great and wonderful he is. Only God can put pretty colors in the sky. We thank God for his glory that shows us how wonderful he is.

Carry On, Cub!

Before you close your eyes tonight, think a little bit about being thankful. God has given us many beautiful things to see. The sky at sunrise and sunset, trees, animals, rivers, and lakes. But sometimes we forget to tell him thank you for such beautiful things to look at. Look around tomorrow. Find three extra special things God has made. Thank him with a prayer or song of praise. Let God know how wonderful you think he is.

<u>Sister's Prayer</u>
Thank you, Father, for my eyes
to see your glory in the skies.

Let us give thanks to God for his gift. It is so great that no one can tell how wonderful it really is! —2 Corinthians 9:15

Two Words

Honey Bear likes to play with the animals in the family manger scene. As the Bear family puts the animals and people around the manger, they talk about Jesus. Do you talk about Jesus at Christmas? He is the reason we have Christmas every year. The gift of Jesus is the greatest gift in the whole world. You might not have enough words to tell how great Jesus is, but there is something you can say. You can tell God thank you for his very special gift. It's only two words!

Carry On, Cub!

Before you close your eyes tonight, think a little bit about being thankful. Never forget to say thank you. It is just two simple words but they mean a lot! Saying thank you shows that you know how special something is. God likes to hear that you think his gifts are special too. He wants to hear you say thank you for Jesus. Then he knows Jesus is in your heart. So say thank you to God tomorrow and every day.

> <u>Honey Bear's Prayer</u>
> *Thank you for Jesus, who came to save.*
> *Thank you, God, for the gift you gave.*

Be Courageous

God gave us his Spirit. And the Spirit doesn't make us weak and fearful. Instead, the Spirit gives us power and love. He helps us control ourselves. —2 Timothy 1:7

Playground Heroes

There's trouble on the playground at Brother and Sister's school. Some bullies are pushing and shoving and name-calling. Brother and Sister are being brave. They are helping their friends so they won't get hurt. Sometimes it's hard to stick up for our friends, and it's easier to not do anything. But if you see someone being treated badly, just ask God to give you his spirit of power and love. God will help you to be a brave helper in times of trouble.

> **Brother's Prayer**
> *If someone's in trouble and starts to shout,*
> *give me courage to help them out.*

Every word of God is perfect. He is like a shield to those who trust in him. He keeps them safe. —Proverbs 30:5

A Safe Place

Honey Bear is looking at the mama owl and her three baby owlets in the tree. They are safe and warm in their cozy nest. When we feel safe, we are not afraid. The Bible tells us that God keeps us safe when we trust him. The more we learn about God through the Bible, the more we will feel safe. God's Word helps us make good choices. It tells us to pray when we are afraid. Being close to God is always the safest place to be.

> *Honey Bear's Prayer*
> *When I'm afraid I'll say a prayer*
> *for you to keep me in your care.*

Do not let your hearts be troubled. And do not be afraid.
—John 14:27

Batter-Up!

Sister is getting ready to bat. She hopes she will hit the ball hard and run all the way to first base. She is not worried or afraid though. She knows God will help her do her best. Playing sports is fun but it can also make you nervous when it's your turn. You want to help your team win the game, but it doesn't always work out that way. Just ask God to help you do your best and to not be afraid—that's what matters most.

Carry On, Cub!

Before you close your eyes tonight, think a little bit about courage. Many people feel a little scared sometime. Maybe there is a big math test. Or an important dance recital. Whatever makes you feel a little scared or nervous, you can pray to God for help. You can ask him to help you be brave. Knowing that God is beside you tomorrow and every day will give you the confidence you need.

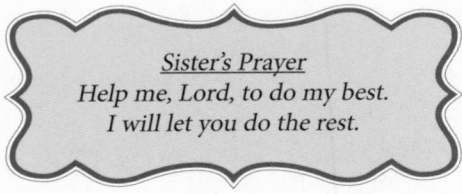

Sister's Prayer
Help me, Lord, to do my best.
I will let you do the rest.

When I'm afraid, I put my trust in you.
—Psalm 56:3

Just Trust

The Bear family is stuck on the side of the road with big car problems. Sister is afraid the car will never restart and they will miss their neighborhood party. She is hoping someone will come along to help them. Sometimes things happen that make us worried or afraid. Everyone gets afraid now and then—even grownups! Just remember God wants you to trust him. Anytime you are afraid you can talk to God and ask him to help you.

Carry On, Cub!

Before you close your eyes tonight, think a little bit about courage. Do you know what trust is? If you have trust in someone you know you can believe that person. God wants us to trust him, he wants us to believe he will take care of us. If something happens that makes you feel afraid, put your trust in God. Say a prayer, asking him to make sure everything turns out the way it should. He will help you.

<u>Sister's Prayer</u>
Jesus, I will trust you today,
no matter what may come my way.

I can do all this by the power of Christ. He gives me strength.
—Philippians 4:13

An Extra Push

Brother, Sister, and Honey Bear are riding their bikes in the big neighborhood parade. Honey is trying hard to keep up. She doesn't want to get left behind. Maybe someone will give her an extra push. When you have something hard to do, you can ask God to give you his power. He will give you the strength to run around the bases or take a spelling test or pedal your bike. When you ask God for help, he will give you strength.

> *Honey Bear's Prayer*
> *Thank you that you make me strong.*
> *Give me your power all day long.*

What should we say then? Since God is on our side, who can be against us? —Romans 8:31

Brother likes the story of David and Goliath. Even though Goliath was a great big giant, David won the battle against Goliath because God was on David's side. If you love Jesus then God is on your side too. He can help you with your giant problems. He is on your side when you stand up to bullies. He can help you do what's right when kids want you to do something wrong. Sometimes it's hard to be brave, but with God on your side you don't need to be afraid.

Brother's Prayer
God, you're always on my side.
You will be my strength and guide.

103

Be strong and brave. Do not be afraid. Do not lose hope. I am the
LORD *your God. I will be with you everywhere you go.*
—Joshua 1:9

Everywhere You Go

Brother and Sister are on their way to school. They
know some bullies might come to tease them. But
they are not afraid. They remember God's promise to
be with them. God tells us in the Bible that we don't
need to be afraid because he is with us everywhere
we go. God is with us at home, but he is also with us
at school or when we are at a friend's house. If you're
ever afraid, just remember God's promise to be with
you everywhere.

Carry On, Cub!

*Before you close your eyes tonight, think a little bit about
courage. God is with you everywhere you go. There is nothing
bigger, stronger, braver, or more loving than God and how he
feels about his children. Tomorrow when you go out to play,
go to school, or church, remember that God is right next to
you. You can count on him to be with you to protect and love
you always and everywhere.*

<u>Sister's Prayer</u>
*Lord, you're with me wherever I go.
Your words in the Bible tell me so.*

There is no fear in love. Instead, perfect love drives away fear. —1 John 4:18

No More Fears

The Bear family is watching an Easter play at church. The play reminds them Easter is not about chocolate bunnies and baskets of candy. Easter is about God's perfect love. God loves us so much he sent his own Son, Jesus, to die on the cross for our sins. If we believe in Jesus then we won't be punished for our sins. You don't ever have to be afraid of God. His perfect love takes away our sins and takes away our fears.

> *Honey Bear's Prayer*
> *Lord, you take my fears away.*
> *Your love is with me every day.*

*LORD, you are my Light and my Savior, so why should
I be afraid of anyone?* —Psalm 27:1

A Happy Ending

Sister likes the ending of the Easter play at Sunday
school. At first the play was a little too scary, but
not anymore. The Easter story has a happy ending.
After Jesus came back to life, he went to heaven. The
Bible says that heaven is a beautiful place. It's always
light in heaven because Jesus is there. Anyone who
believes in Jesus can be with him in heaven someday.
When Jesus is your Savior, you do not have to be
afraid. Your life will have a happy ending too.

> *Sister's Prayer*
> *You are my Light and Savior too.*
> *Someday I'll live in heaven with you.*

Let the Lord make you strong. Depend on his mighty power. —Ephesians 6:10

Strong and Mighty

Brother, Sister, and Honey Bear are getting a big bear hug from Grizzly Gramps. He is strong enough to hold all of them at the same time. Some grownups are very strong, but kids can be strong too. You might not be able to lift three people, but God can make you strong on the inside. Then you can do what is right. The next time you are tempted to do something wrong, ask God to give you his strength and power to make the right choices.

Carry On, Cub!

Before you close your eyes tonight, think a little bit about courage. Sometimes being brave doesn't have to do with our bodies and how powerful we are. Sometimes being brave has to do with our thoughts and how strong our brains and feeling are. God helps you to be brave in all ways. So if you need to make a choice that seems hard or scary, ask God for help tomorrow. He will give you the courage to make the right choice.

> ### Brother's Prayer
> *Help me to be brave and strong,*
> *to do what's right instead of wrong.*

Be A Good Friend

Two people are better than one. They can help each other in everything they do. —Ecclesiastes 4:9

A Tangled Mess

Lizzy was trying to catch a fish, but her fishing line got all tangled. Sister was fishing too, but she stopped to help her friend. Now they are working together to get Lizzy's line untangled. That's what good friends do. If one of your friends is having a problem, you can stop what you are doing and help your friend. Even if you are doing something fun, it's more important to help. Two people can fix a problem better than one, and maybe someday that friend will help you.

> <u>Sister's Prayer</u>
> *Even if I'm having fun,*
> *give me strength to help someone.*

An honest witness does not lie.
—Proverbs 14:5

Tell the Truth

Sister is arguing with Brother. She doesn't believe
what he is saying. She thinks he is making things up.
When you say something that is not true, it's called
a lie. The Bible warns us about lying. When you tell
a lie, it can cause a whole lot of trouble. You would
never want someone to lie to you, so be sure you
never lie to your friends or family. It's always best to
be honest and tell the truth—no matter what.

Brother's Prayer
Help me, Lord, to say what's true
to all my friends and family too.

Love is patient. Love is kind.
—1 Corinthians 13:4

Patient and Kind

Brother and Sister are being patient and kind while they wait for the school bell to ring. They are not pushing or shoving to be first in line. Sometimes it's hard to be patient and kind, but that's what God wants us to do. You can be patient and kind by letting others go ahead of you in line. You can be patient and kind by being a good listener when someone tells you a story. When you are patient and kind, you are being a good friend!

Carry On, Cub!

Before you close your eyes tonight, think a little bit about friendship. How can you be a good friend? Just like Brother and Sister you can treat others with kindness and caring. You can be helpful and a good listener. You can be friendly and patient. If you act this way you are being the kind of friend Jesus was on earth. Tomorrow, make it a goal to be a friend like that.

> <u>Sister's Prayer</u>
> *With all my heart and all my mind,*
> *I'll be a friend who's patient and kind.*

*Here is my command. Love one another,
just as I have loved you. —John 15:12*

Love Like Jesus

Honey Bear is running around with Brother and Sister and their friends. She is happy the bigger cubs are letting her play with them. Jesus wants us to be a good friend to everyone. He loves us all the same. It doesn't matter how big or small you are, or what color hair you have. It doesn't matter where you live. Jesus loves you just the way you are, and he wants you to love others that way too.

Carry On, Cub!

Before you close your eyes tonight, think a little bit about friendship. What makes a good friend? Is it how tall someone is, how good someone is at playing baseball, or what color hair someone has? NO! God loves everyone no matter what. And that is what he wants us to do too. Tomorrow be a good friend like Jesus was on earth. Include everyone in a game on the playground. Introduce yourself to a new classmate. Try to love everyone.

<u>Honey Bear's Prayer</u>
*Lord, you love us all the same.
Bless my friends in Jesus' name.*

A friend loves at all times. They are there to help when trouble comes. —Proverbs 17:17

All the Time

Brother sees his friend getting hurt on the playground. He runs over to help. Friends are there in good times and bad. It's fun to play tag with your friends or swing on the swings together. But when one of your friends is having a problem, that's when you can show what a good friend you really are. You can see if your friend is hurt, or find a grownup to help. You can be a good friend all the time.

> *Brother's Prayer*
> *Thank you for times to play and run,*
> *and times when I can help someone.*

None of you should look out just for your own good.
Each of you should also look out for the good of others.
—Philippians 2:4

Look Out For Others

Sister likes to look out the window when she rides
the bus to school. But today she is looking at the
girl in the seat behind her. Sister thinks Suzie might
be worried about something. She wants to be sure
Suzie is okay. Do you look out for others at home
or school? You might be having a good day, but
someone else might be having a bad day. When you
look out for someone else, you can both have a good
day.

> *Sister's Prayer*
> *Help me, Lord, to look and see*
> *when someone else is needing me.*

[Love] does not brag. It is not proud.
1 Corinthians 13:4

No More Bragging

Brother thinks he is smarter than Sister. Sister thinks she is smarter than Brother. Sometimes they brag about how good they are at soccer. Bragging comes from being proud. Kids who brag often think they are better than other kids. Instead of bragging about yourself, you can tell your friends, "Good job!" when they score a goal or get an A on a test. When you make your friends feel good about themselves, you will have a good feeling too. You are doing the right thing.

Carry On, Cub!

Before you close your eyes tonight, think a little bit about friendship. When a friend does great at a ball game or writes a funny story you like, do you remember to say, "Good job"? It is important to let friends know when they do something well. It makes them feel happy and it will make you feel happy too when you see your friend smile!

> *Brother's Prayer*
> *Help me to make my friends feel good*
> *and treat them just the way I should.*

You are my friends if you do what I command.
—John 15:14

A Special Friend

Sister is playing with a new friend she met at the park. His name is Tommy. She hopes they will be special friends. It's nice to have friends to play with, but Jesus is the most special friend you can have. You can talk to him all the time. He listens to you and loves you no matter what. Jesus wants you to learn about him by reading the Bible. He wants you to obey his words and be blessed. That's how you can be a friend of Jesus.

Carry On, Cub!

Before you close your eyes tonight, think a little bit about friendship. Jesus is a friend to everyone. He was born so that all people could learn how to be a good friend from him. He treated everyone he met with respect. That is how we should be too. Starting tomorrow try to be a good friend like Jesus. Read the Bible to find out how he showed his friends he loved them. Try living like him.

Sister's Prayer
Jesus, you're my special friend.
Thank you for the love you send.

Suppose either of them falls down. Then the one can help the other one up. —Ecclesiastes 4:10

Getting Back Up

Sister was knocked down during the soccer game. Now Brother is making sure she is all right. Sometimes Brother and Sister annoy each other, but sometimes they are good friends. If you have a brother or sister, you can be friends too. Whether your friends are in your neighborhood, at school, or right in your home, you can show your love by caring about them. If someone falls down, you can be a good friend and help them get back up.

Carry On, Cub!

Before you close your eyes tonight, think a little more about friendship. Friends and brothers and sisters help one another. It's kind of a rule that family and friends are helpful and kind to each other. So if you have a friend that falls down, drops something, or loses something, you should really help out. Jesus was the best friend ever. He showed us through his example that helping out is what we should do—there are stories in the Bible about Jesus curing the blind man, helping a man who couldn't stand up, and even bringing a girl back to life! We cannot do miracles like that for our friends but we can help them tomorrow and every day.

Brother's Prayer
When friends are running all around,
I'll help someone who might fall down.

Love one another deeply. Honor others more than yourselves. —Romans 12:10

Love and Honor

Sister is fishing with Brother and their neighborhood friends. She likes it when everyone gets along. They are being good friends and showing love to each other. The Bible tells us to love and honor others. You can do that by treating others with kindness. You can be a friend who cares about others and cheers them up when they are sad. When you love and honor others, you are being the kind of friend God wants you to be.

Carry On, Cub!

Before you close your eyes tonight, think a little bit about friendship. You want to have good friends. You want friends that make you laugh and that you can have fun with and talk to. You want good friends that help and support you and cheer you up when you are sad. So starting tomorrow you need to try being that kind of friend to someone else. When you love and support others the way God wants you to, they will love and be kind to you.

<u>Sister's Prayer</u>
*Thank you for friends who are good to me
the kind of friend that I want to be.*

Have Faith

The commandments I give you today
must be in your hearts. —Deuteronomy 6:6

In Your Heart

Papa likes reading Bible stories to Brother and Sister at bedtime. The Bible has many exciting stories. But the Bible is more than just a storybook. The Bible tells the big story of God's love and how he sent Jesus to save us from our sins. It also has some good instructions that help us make wise choices so we can be happy and safe. God wants us to keep those instructions in our hearts and minds. They will help us and guide us each day.

Sister's Prayer
Put your words inside my heart.
Oh, Lord, please fill up every part.

Trust in the LORD with all your heart. Do not depend on your own understanding. —Proverbs 3:5

Depend on God

Honey Bear is happy she can ride her bike with Brother and Sister. She doesn't know if today is going to be a happy day or a sad day, but she is going to trust God and not worry. No one knows what will happen from one day to the next. Some days are happy and some are not. But you can trust that God knows what is best. You can depend on him to care for you every day because he loves you.

> *Honey Bear's Prayer*
> *I trust you, Lord, and understand*
> *that every day is in your hand.*

We live by believing, not by seeing.
—2 Corinthians 5:7

Just Believe

The Bear family is about to eat a delicious lunch. But first, they are saying a prayer to thank God for their food and friends. Do you remember to pray at mealtime and bedtime? Do you talk to God when you are at home or school? When you pray, you are talking to a real God who can hear you. Even though you cannot see God, he sees you. The Bible tells us God is real. You don't need to see God to know he is real, you just need to believe.

Carry On, Cub!

Before you close your eyes tonight, think a little bit about faith. Prayer is important. It is a way to talk with God. You can pray every day, all day. You can pray at mealtime, bedtime, on the bus, in the kitchen, and at the playground. God is always listening and ready to help. Think about praying tomorrow. Not just at the "normal" times like at dinner and bedtime. But pray on your way to school and when you are helping with the dishes. God likes to hear from you!

<u>Brother's Prayer</u>
Lord, I know that you are there.
You hear me when I say a prayer.

Let us keep looking to Jesus. He is the one who started this journey of faith. And he is the one who completes the journey of faith. —Hebrews 12:2

Look to Jesus

The Bears enjoy the Christmas Eve pageant at the Chapel in the Woods. Some cubs from Brother and Sister's Sunday school are playing the three wise men this year. They are following the star as they look for Jesus. In Bible times, people waited for Jesus to come because God promised he would send a Savior. Even though Jesus came to earth a long time ago, we still look to him to be our friend and helper and Savior. If you look for Jesus, you will find him.

Carry On, Cub!

Before you close your eyes tonight, think a little bit about faith. Jesus came to earth to be our friend and Savior. God made a promise and he kept that promise. Today we do not have a star to help us find Jesus like the wise men had. But we have the Bible to help guide us and we have our faith. If we believe that Jesus is our Savior we will be in heaven with him. Look for Jesus tomorrow … read the story of his birth in the Bible.

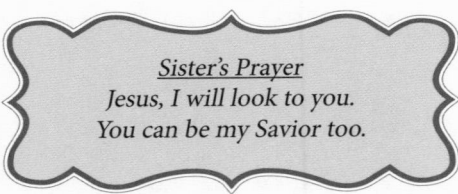

Sister's Prayer
Jesus, I will look to you.
You can be my Savior too.

*Jesus Christ is the same yesterday
and today and forever. —Hebrews 13:8*

Always the Same

The cubs are enjoying a beautiful fall day. Brother,
Sister, and Honey Bear like to toss the colorful leaves
into the air and watch them fall. Did you know that
fall always comes after summer, and winter always
comes after fall? Every year it's always the same,
and it does not change. Jesus is always the same too.
Jesus is our Lord and Savior and friend. He watches
over you and cares for you. His love for you will
never change. It will last forever.

> *Honey Bear's Prayer*
> *Winter, summer, spring, or fall,
> you are always Lord of all.*

Don't let anyone look down on you because you are young.
Set an example for the believers in what you say
and in how you live. —1 Timothy 4:12

Not Too Young

Brother is learning to play a song on his guitar. He is still too young to be a famous music star, but he is practicing so he can get better. Kids have to wait until they are older to do certain things, but there are many things they can do even while they are young. If you believe in Jesus, you can be a good example to your friends and family. You can share and be kind. And most of all, you can tell your friends about Jesus.

Brother's Prayer
Jesus, I don't have to wait
to tell my friends that you are great!

*So in Christ Jesus you are all children of
God by believing in Christ. —Galatians 3:26*

Children of God

Brother and Sister like it when their friends get
along. Sometimes their friends get into arguments,
but Brother and Sister try to be the peacemakers.
God wants his children to get along with each other
too. Did you know you can be a child of God?
Anyone who believes in Jesus is a child of God.
God's children are like brothers and sisters because
God is their father. You can be a child of God if you
believe in Jesus. You can be part of God's big family.

Carry On, Cub!

*Before you close your eyes tonight, think a little bit about faith.
We are all brothers and sisters in Christ. Because of our faith,
we belong to the same family, a family led by God the Father!
This is a family that is built on love and is a family that will
always be there for us. As you work and play tomorrow, thank
God that you are a part of his family. Prayer helps keep your
faith strong, so pray!*

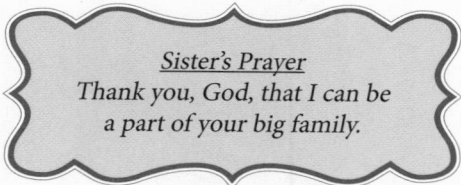

Sister's Prayer
*Thank you, God, that I can be
a part of your big family.*

*Trust in the L*ORD* forever. The L*ORD* himself is the Rock.
The L*ORD* will keep us safe forever. —Isaiah 26:4*

God is Our Rock

Preacher Brown is reminding Brother, Sister, and
their friends that God is the one who keeps us safe
when we trust in him. When troubles come, we can
ask God for his help. God is never too busy to listen
to your prayers. The Bible says that God is our rock.
That means he is strong and mighty. God can do
anything. The next time you need help, remember—
God is always there to help you and keep you safe.

> *Brother's Prayer*
> *Lord, when troubles come my way,*
> *I will turn to you and pray.*

LORD who rules over all, blessed is the person who trusts in you. —Psalm 84:12

Ruler of All

Honey Bear loves going for a walk with Mama and Papa. They are looking at all the things God created. He made the rocks and trees, the pond and plants. He made the frogs that jump, the ducks that quack, and the fish that splash. God rules over everything he made and takes good care of his creation. God is our creator and ruler. Anyone who believes in God can see his greatness in the things he made. People who trust in God are blessed.

> *Honey Bear's Prayer*
> *I know you made the things I see—*
> *the rocks and trees and even me.*

Let the message about Christ live among you like a rich treasure. Teach and correct one another wisely. —Colossians 3:16

Something to Treasure

Mama and Papa are giving Sister a beautiful golden locket for her birthday. The Golden Rule is written inside the locket. Sister will take good care of her locket and keep it as a special treasure. The Bible is a special treasure too. It tells us about God and how much he loves us. The Bible teaches us how to live and how to treat others. People who believe in God know how special the Bible is. It is something to treasure!

Carry On, Cub!

Before you close your eyes tonight, think a little bit about faith. The Bible teaches us about our faith. It has stories about faithful people that we can use as examples in our lives. It has rules that we can follow that help make our faith stronger, like the Golden Rule and the Ten Commandments. If we have the gift of faith in God, we believe that he is the source of all love.

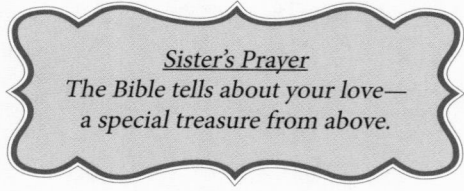

Sister's Prayer
*The Bible tells about your love—
a special treasure from above.*

Be Joyful

Always be joyful because you belong to the Lord.
—Philippians 4:4

Jump for Joy

Brother and Sister Bear are jumping in a big pile of leaves. They are full of joy as they play outdoors on a beautiful day. Joy is a good feeling you have deep down inside. People have joy for many reasons. You might have joy when you make a new friend or move to a new neighborhood. The best reason to have joy is that God loves you. When you remember how much God loves you, you can have joy all day, every day.

> <u>Brother's Prayer</u>
> *Thank you, Father, for the joy*
> *you give to every girl and boy.*

How you made me is amazing and wonderful.
I praise you for that. —Psalm 139:14

Amazing Things

Sister loves to paint pretty pictures. She is happy God made her in such an amazing way. You are amazing too! Do like to paint or draw? Maybe you like to put jigsaw puzzles together or play games. God made your body so you can move. He made your mind so you can think and learn. He gave you a voice so you can talk and laugh and sing. Whatever you enjoy doing, praise God that you are able to do so many amazing things.

> *Sister's Prayer*
> *You made me in a wonderful way.*
> *Thank you for things I can do each day.*

*Clap your hands, all you nations. Shout to God with cries of joy.
Do this because the LORD Most High is wonderful.
He is the great King over the whole earth. —Psalm 47:1-2*

Clap Your Hands

The Bear family is singing and clapping their hands. They are filled with joy because they went to church and Sunday school to learn more about God. God is great and wonderful. He is the King of the whole earth. God is in control of everything so we don't have to worry. We can be full of joy and sing praises to God because he is our Lord. The more you learn about God, the more joy you will have in your heart!

Carry On, Cub!

Before you close your eyes tonight, think a little bit about joy. Joy is more than just feeling happy. Joy is a huge feeling of love in your heart that makes you want to clap and sing and maybe even dance! Where does joy come from? Joy comes from being really sure that God loves you and is taking care of you. Joy comes from knowing as much as you can about how much God cares. Tomorrow take some time and ask mom or dad about what brings them joy.

<u>Honey Bear's Prayer</u>
*I'll shout for joy, I'll clap and sing.
The Lord Most High is God and King.*

*The Lord has done it on this day. Let us
be joyful today and be glad.* —Psalm 118:24

Be Glad

Today is the day of the big Harvest Festival! The Bear
family and their friends are excited to enjoy juicy
apples, pumpkin pie, and a hayride. Some days are
extra special—like birthdays and Thanksgiving and
Christmas. But when you love God, every day can
be that special. Every day is a gift from God. It might
not always be a day with fancy food or hayrides. But
God's love makes every day worth living. You can be
glad today because God loves you.

Carry On, Cub!

*Before you close your eyes tonight, think a little bit about joy.
Can you always feel joy? Yes, you can! Tomorrow, look around
you and find five things God has brought into your life that
bring you great happiness—joy. Maybe it is your little baby
brother. Maybe you get joy from jumping in puddles. Maybe
you feel joy when you read a book. All good things in your life
are from God—he loves you. Be joyful all day!*

> ### Sister's Prayer
> *Every day is a gift from you.
> I will be glad and joyful too!*

You always show me the path of life. You will fill me with joy when I am with you. —Psalm 16:11

Follow the Path

Brother is excited because he sees a deer. He loves walking with his family down the path to Farmer Ben's farm. Paths are fun to follow because you never know what you will see along the way. You might see furry animals or pretty stones or tiny bugs. Life is a lot like walking a path. Every day is another step on the path and you never know what might happen. But when you know that God will guide your steps, you can enjoy following the path.

> *Brother's Prayer*
> *Thank you, God, that you're my guide.*
> *I want to stay close by your side.*

Praise the LORD. . . . Praise him because he is greater than anything else. Praise him by blowing trumpets. —Psalm 150:1-3

Loud Praises

Mama Bear is playing her trumpet and Brother and Sister think it's too loud! Music can make us feel joyful, but sometimes it can be too loud. When it comes to praising God, music can be loud or soft or somewhere in between. The Bible says to praise God with loud trumpets because he is so great. Do you like to praise God? We can praise God by singing or playing instruments. Any kind of music that praises God is joyful music to his ears.

> <u>Sister's Prayer</u>
> *Jesus, there are many ways*
> *to bring to you a song of praise.*

Good things come to those who do what is right.
Joy comes to those whose hearts are honest. —Psalm 97:11

A Good Reward

Brother is wearing a big smile on his face. He became a member of the Bear Country Rocket Club. He was extra nice to a younger cub. Being kind and loving is always the right thing to do. Even if no one else sees the good things you do, God sees, and that's what matters most. Treating others the right way will make you feel good inside. It will put joy deep inside your heart—and that's the best reward of all!

Carry On, Cub!

Before you close your eyes tonight, think a little bit about joy. If you have joy are you always singing, dancing, smiling, and clapping? No, joy can be quiet and in your heart too. Joy comes from knowing how much God loves you—and he loves you when you do loud and happy things like singing his praise. But he also loves you when you help your sister learn her spelling words or when you pick up the toys in your room. Tomorrow, do a good deed—and think about the smile you just put on God's face!

<u>Brother's Prayer</u>
Help me to do what's right, oh Lord.
Having joy is my reward.

Sing a new song to the LORD. All you people of the earth, sing to the LORD. —Psalm 96:1

Sing For Joy

The Bear family is riding in a sleigh through the countryside. They are on their way to Grizzly Gramps and Gran's house. They are singing because they are happy. Being with your family is a good reason to be happy, but God gives us lots of other reasons to be happy too. Even if you are not feeling happy, it's good to sing praises to God anyway. If you start to sing, you just might get a smile on your face!

<u>Honey Bear's Prayer</u>
Thank you for happy songs to sing.
Thank you for the joy you bring.

Let the heavens be full of joy.
Let the earth be glad. —Psalm 96:11

All Year Long

The sun is shining in the sky as Mama, Papa, Brother, Sister, and Honey Bear walk to church. It's a crisp winter morning with sparkling snow on the ground. When you are outdoors, you can see beautiful things God created. Whether it's summer or winter, spring or fall, God's creation shows us how great and mighty he is. God's creation shouts his name all year long! God's glory is all around us. All we need to do is look around to enjoy it.

> <u>Sister's Prayer</u>
> *Every season it's the same—*
> *All creation shouts your name.*

Then I will be full of joy because of what the L<small>ORD</small> has done. I will be glad because he has saved me. —Psalm 35:9

Preacher Brown is reading from the Bible as the Bear family listens. It's important to listen when someone reads the Bible. We can learn many things. We can learn about God's love and how to be saved from our sins. We can learn how to show love to others by being kind. The Bible gives us wisdom that will help us make good choices. And the more we listen to God's Word, the more joy we will have. Do you want to have joy? Listen to God's Word!

Carry On, Cub!

Before you close your eyes tonight, think a little bit about joy. Some people do not have joy in their lives. They do not know about God's love and how he saved us from our sins. Tomorrow, promise that you will make good choices. Promise that everything you do will show your friends and other people God is with you and that you are filled with joy. Pray that through your example, someone might see your joy and want that too. Pray that someone new will find joy in Christ.

> <u>Brother's Prayer</u>
> *Your word, oh Lord, will be my guide.*
> *It gives me joy deep down inside.*